Respecting the Contributions of
Asian Americans

Anna Kingston

PowerKiDS press™

New York

Published in 2013 by The Rosen Publishing Group, Inc.
29 East 21st Street, New York, NY 10010

First Edition

Editor: Jennifer Way
Book Design: Erica Clendening and Ashley Drago
Layout Design: Andrew Povolny

Photo Credits: Cover, p. 4 Alexander Nemenov/AFP/Getty Images; p. 5 Paul Hawthorne/Getty Images; p. 6 © iStockphoto.com/Jodi Matthews; p. 7 Dawn Shearer-Simonetti/Shutterstock.com; p. 8 SeanPavonePhoto/Shutterstock.com; p. 9 Mario Tama/Getty Images; p. 10 Kean Collection/Archive Photos/Getty Images; p. 11 Ethan Miller/Getty Images; p. 12 Russell Shively/Shutterstock.com; p. 13 Buyenlarge/Archive Photos/Getty Images; p. 14 Time Life Pictures/Getty Images; p. 15 Marco Garcia/Getty Images; p. 17 Kevork Djansezian/Getty Images; up. 18 Justin Sullivan/Getty Images; p. 19 Jon Kopaloff/FilmMagic/Getty Images; p. 20 Jean-Claude LABBE/Gamma-Rapho/Getty Images; p. 21 Bloomberg/Getty Images; p. 22 Ariel Skelley/Blend Images.

Library of Congress Cataloging-in-Publication Data

Kingston, Anna.
 Respecting the contributions of Asian Americans / by Anna Kingston. — 1st ed.
     p. cm. — (Stop bullying now!)
 Includes index.
 ISBN 978-1-4488-7447-7 (library binding) — ISBN 978-1-4488-7520-7 (pbk.) — ISBN 978-1-4488-7594-8 (6-pack)
 1. Asian Americans—History—Juvenile literature. 2. Asians—United States—History—Juvenile literature. I. Title.
 E184.A75K57 2013
 973'.0495—dc23
                                    2012003977

Manufactured in the United States of America

CPSIA Compliance Information: Batch #SW12PK: For Further Information contact Rosen Publishing, New York, New York at 1-800-237-9932

Contents

Making Their Mark

Asian Americans are Americans whose families have their roots in Asia. They have made their marks in many fields. Jerry Yang helped found the search engine Yahoo!. M. Night Shyamalan is a movie director, while Brenda Song is an actress. Kristi Yamaguchi, Michelle Kwan, and Richard Park have all wowed people on the ice. Yamaguchi and Kwan are figure skaters, while Park plays ice hockey.

Leroy Chiao is an engineer and former astronaut. He is Chinese American.

I. M. Pei is a world-famous architect. He was born in China and became a US citizen as an adult.

Even though Asian Americans have done great things, they have faced **prejudice** from other Americans. Some have said Asian Americans are not "real Americans." Others tried to stop people from Asia from moving to the United States.

Facing Bullying

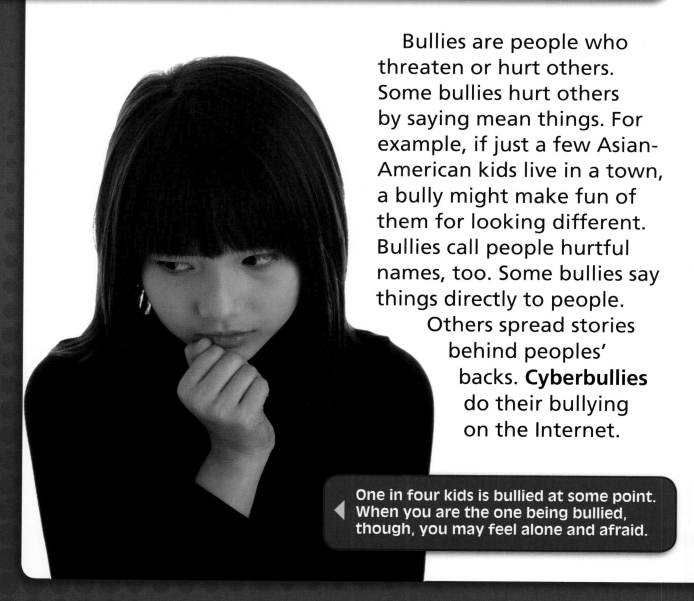

Bullies are people who threaten or hurt others. Some bullies hurt others by saying mean things. For example, if just a few Asian-American kids live in a town, a bully might make fun of them for looking different. Bullies call people hurtful names, too. Some bullies say things directly to people. Others spread stories behind peoples' backs. **Cyberbullies** do their bullying on the Internet.

One in four kids is bullied at some point. When you are the one being bullied, though, you may feel alone and afraid.

A kid who is being bullied may have a hard time standing up for herself. You can help by speaking up or talking to a trusted adult about the bullying.

People who beat up other kids are bullies. People who threaten to do so are as well. **Exclusion** is bullying, too. Teachers, parents, and other trusted adults can help students who are being bullied.

Asia is Earth's biggest **continent,** or big landmass. It is also the continent with the biggest **population,** or number of people living on it. Asia is home to many countries, each with its own history and rich **culture**. A culture is the beliefs, practices, and arts of a group of people.

Many large American cities have thriving Asian-American communities. This is Chinatown in New York City.

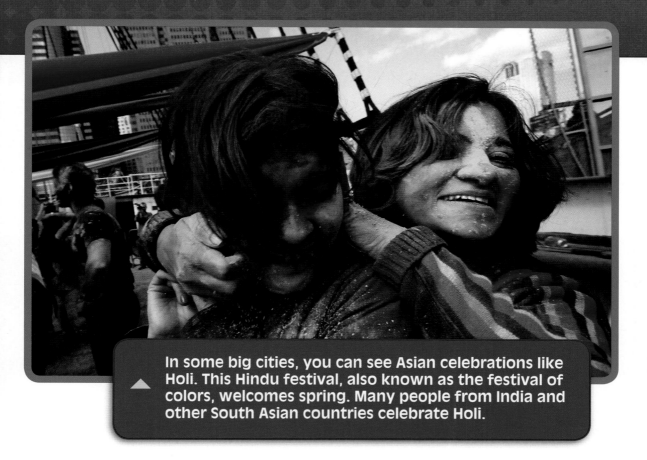

In some big cities, you can see Asian celebrations like Holi. This Hindu festival, also known as the festival of colors, welcomes spring. Many people from India and other South Asian countries celebrate Holi.

In spite of their differences, Americans with roots in China, Japan, Korea, the Philippines, Southeast Asia, India, and other Asian countries are all Asian Americans. While some Asian Americans were born in Asia, others come from families that have lived in the United States for **generations**.

Some of the earliest Asian Americans were **immigrants** who came to the United States from China during the gold rush in California in the 1840s. In the 1860s, more Chinese immigrants came to work on the

The Chinese immigrants who worked on the Central Pacific Railroad did not all come directly from China. Many had come to California to work during the gold rush.

transcontinental railroad. This railroad linked the East Coast to the West Coast. More than 10,000 Chinese immigrants worked on the Central Pacific Railroad, which ran through the Sierra Nevada, a mountain chain in California.

Though the Chinese workers worked hard, they were often treated unfairly and were paid less than other workers. Their jobs were dangerous, and they worked long hours on mountainsides.

Steven Chu (1948–)

Physicist Steven Chu is Chinese American. Physicists study energy and matter, or stuff that takes up space. In 1997, Chu won a big honor called the Nobel Prize in Physics. In 2009, he became the secretary of energy. He helps the government use science to meet the country's energy needs.

The Asian-American population grew as the country took over new territories. During the Spanish-American War, the United States invaded the Philippines, which was then ruled by Spain. The Americans won and took over the Philippines in 1898. The Philippines fought for independence from the United States but lost. The Philippines remained a US territory until 1946. During this period, many Filipinos moved to the United States.

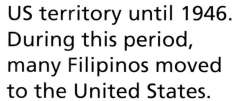

Queen Liliuokalani, shown on this stamp, was the last ruler of the Kingdom of Hawaii. Hawaii then became a US territory.

This painting shows the 1899 Battle of Manila, in which the Philippines fought for independence from the United States.

BATTLE OF PACEO (MANILA) FEBY 4 & 5 1899.

The United States also took over Hawaii in 1898. The islands became home to many people who came from China, Japan, Korea, and the Philippines to work on sugarcane **plantations**, or big farms.

Internment Camps

These Japanese Americans were among the thousands who were sent to internment camps during World War II.

In 1941, the United States entered World War II after Japanese planes bombed Pearl Harbor, Hawaii. During the war, many Americans wrongly believed that Japanese Americans would be loyal to Japan.

The US government rounded up about 120,000 Japanese Americans and put them in **internment camps**. These were in hard-to-reach places. They had armed guards to make sure people could not escape.

In fact, the people in the camps were loyal Americans. Some even had family members who were serving in the US military. The US government finally apologized for its actions in 1988.

Daniel Inouye (1924–)

Daniel Inouye was one of several thousand Japanese Americans who fought in World War II. He lost an arm in the war. He received the Medal of Honor, the highest US military honor, for his service. Inouye was elected to the Senate in 1962. He continues to represent Hawaii today.

In the nineteenth and early twentieth centuries, US laws allowed only a very small number of Asian immigrants to enter the country. In 1965, the Immigration and Nationality Act opened the doors for more Asian immigrants.

Many of the new immigrants came from South Korea. Americans and South Koreans had fought alongside each other in the Korean War during the 1950s, so there were already ties between the countries. Many Korean Americans opened small businesses. Korean Americans did well in other fields, too. Reporters K. W. Lee and Jeannie Park are Korean American.

This girl is showing off a certificate that shows she is an American citizen after a citizenship ceremony in Los Angeles.

Though a handful of immigrants from India came to the United States before the 1960s, most Indian Americans arrived in the later twentieth century. By 2000, the country was home to 1.7 million Indian Americans. In fact, the Indian-American population in 2000 was five times what it was in 1980.

Bobby Jindal's parents came to the United States from India. He grew up in Baton Rouge, Louisiana.

Some Indian Americans moved from India. Others came from Caribbean islands where their families had lived since the nineteenth century. Indian Americans are the most educated group of immigrants. They have done many great things. In 2007, Bobby Jindal was elected the governor of Louisiana. He became the country's first Indian-American governor.

Mindy Kaling (1979–)

Mindy Kaling is an Indian-American actress and writer. Her full name is Vera Mindy Chokalingam. She writes for the TV show *The Office*. She also plays a character named Kelly Kapoor on the show. In 2011, her best-selling book, *Is Everyone Hanging Out Without Me?*, came out.

Fleeing War

Between 1961 and 1973, the United States fought in the Vietnam War. The US military supported the South Vietnamese against the North Vietnamese. It did so because North Vietnam had a form of government called **Communism**, which the United States was against. After the Americans and South Vietnamese lost the war, many people who had sided with them fled the country.

At the end of the Vietnam War, many Vietnamese left their homeland for the United States.

In the following years, more people from Vietnam and other Southeast Asian countries, such as Cambodia and Laos, immigrated to the United States. Many of these immigrants were fleeing troubles in their home countries, too. Others just hoped for better lives.

Joseph Cao was the first Vietnamese American to serve in Congress. He represented Louisiana in the House of Representatives from 2009 until 2011.

Living Together

Asian Americans from a range of backgrounds make the United States a more interesting place to live. However, there are still people who are prejudiced against Asian Americans. If these people do not know how to say Asian Americans' names, they make fun of their names. Other people make fun of how Asian Americans look or talk.

Make sure bullies do not get away with targeting Asian Americans. Stand up for fellow Americans of all backgrounds!

Learning about the different Asian-American groups who have come to the United States helps you understand and respect their contributions to American history.

Glossary

Communism (KOM-yuh-nih-zem) A system in which the government owns all property and goods, which are shared equally by everyone.

continent (KON-tuh-nent) One of Earth's seven large landmasses.

culture (KUL-chur) The beliefs, practices, and arts of a group of people.

cyberbullies (SY-ber-bu-leez) People who do hurtful or threatening things to other people using the Internet.

exclusion (eks-KLOO-zhun) Keeping or shutting someone out.

generations (jeh-nuh-RAY-shunz) Groups of people who are born in the same period.

immigrants (IH-muh-grunts) People who move to a new country from another country.

internment camps (in-TERN-ment KAMPS) Large areas where people who are believed to be dangerous are held, often during a war.

plantations (plan-TAY-shunz) Very large farms where crops are grown.

population (pop-yoo-LAY-shun) A group of people living in the same place.

prejudice (PREH-juh-dis) Disliking a group of people different from you.

transcontinental (trants-kon-tuh-NEN-tul) Going across a continent.

Index

Websites

Due to the changing nature of Internet links, PowerKids Press has developed an online list of websites related to the subject of this book. This site is updated regularly. Please use this link to access the list:
www.powerkidslinks.com/sbn/asian/